Time You Let Me In

25 POETS UNDER 25

What Is Confidence?

Today we will do nothing
or anything, she said, and then
I added, it depends on the wind.
There are swerves
in everything, in the trees
and likewise in the clouds.
Tomorrow will come
no doubt with some surprise
or another. But for now raise the blinds,
there are windows in everything
wide the sky
a perfect blue.

ALEXIS D. PEPPER-SMITH

Time You Let Me In

25 POETS UNDER 25

SELECTED BY
NAOMI SHIHAB NYE

GREENWILLOW BOOKS
An Imprint of HarperCollins Publishers

Naomi Shihab Nye thanks Virginia Duncan, Paul Zakris, and all the staff at Greenwillow Books. With gratitude to Tassajara Zen Mountain Center; Abbot Ryushin Paul Haller and Dana Velden; Hope College in Holland, Michigan; Seeds of Peace; and Bobbie Gottschalk. Special thanks to Carrie Fountain, Barbara Stafford Wilson, Jim Haba, the Dodge Poetry Festival, Samina Najmi, Alex Espinoza, and girls named Lauren.

Time You Let Me In: 25 Poets Under 25
Copyright © 2010 by Naomi Shihab Nye

Page 231 constitutes an extension of this copyright page.

The text of this book is set in 12-point Bembo.
Book design by Paul Zakris

Library of Congress Cataloging-in-Publication Data
Time you let me in : 25 poets under 25 / selected by Naomi Shihab Nye.
p. cm.
"Greenwillow Books."
Includes bibliographical references and index.
ISBN 978-0-06-189637-8 (trade bdg.) — ISBN 978-0-06-189638-5 (lib. bdg.)
1. American poetry—21st century. I. Nye, Naomi Shihab.
PS617.T56 2009   811'.608—dc22   2009019387

11 12 13 14 CG/RRDB 10 9 8 7 6 5
First Edition

 Greenwillow Books

To Jack Ridl,
encouraging friend of young poets
the wide world over

CONTENTS

x

INTRODUCTION

If you drive old farm road 43 from Corpus Christi, Texas, up
to Driscoll right at dawn and for the thirty minutes or so after-
ward, through the tiny towns of London and Petronila, past
the cotton gins and weather-beaten farmhouses and few stop
signs and blinking red lights, past the mysterious old tractors,
some shrouded under tarps, some parked right where they
stopped working, you'll sometimes see a soft haze or mist. A
vast horizontal cloud of fog in all directions, rising from the
amazingly flat earth into the air, but hovering—as if the old
fields are breathing. The breath connecting earth and sky . . .
after a quiet, mysterious night of winking stars and wind from
the bay, the fields are turning over in their rumpled soil beds.
The breath of the ages is rising. And you are inside it.

There is something so companionable about this mysterious time of day, which I first witnessed as a twenty-three-

year-old, driving to conduct poetry workshops at H. M. King High School in Kingsville. Those hopeful silent fields could almost signify an entire coming-of-age period of life. Magical awakening, a little spooky, doesn't last long—sometimes difficult on the vision—did we miss the turn? Are we on the right road? Late teens, early twenties—we feel our childhood possibilities realizing themselves in whatever experimental first jobs we find and awkward/graceful moves we make, earth and sky so connected. We tell ourselves, *Take a deep breath—hold on*—will we be able to do it? Will adulthood welcome us, too, along with all our friends? Where are they right now?

We pause even when there isn't a rest stop—what can't we stand to leave behind? What astonishing surprises are about to unfold? How will language carry us along, rolling, rolling, on the old blacktop, as we pull onto the shoulder for a moment of pause and observation while all the speedier cars and pickups barrel by?

Reading the poems for *Time You Let Me In* reminded me of the sensation of vast horizontal breathing. The voices of these wonderful writers open up into whole worlds of roots and rumpled sleep and radiant dreaming. There's hope here, and humor, and snazzy intelligence. No matter what age we are, we need these voices. I remember my own son teaching me how to use a computer—when he was three—and think of how these sharp poets grew up in a sizzling world of computer and high-tech information—for sure—but they're still timeless in their passions, interests, complications, and devotions. They have much to report and remind us of. As the writer Sandra Cisneros once said, we all carry all our ages within us—somewhere deep inside in there, every older person is still seven . . .

and seventeen . . . and, we might wonder, is it possible we're all carrying an eighty-year-old, too?

There's a grapefruit stand at Driscoll where trucks from the Texas Valley unload huge mountains of fresh citrus daily—succulent ruby red grapefruits, perfect plump oranges, a new kind of giant lemon—onto crooked wooden tables, into cardboard bins. That's the feeling of being in one's twenties, sometimes—so much to pick from—how will we do it? If we buy this entire sack of grapefruits, will we be able to eat them in time before they spoil? Can we give half of them away?

Poet Anna West wrote,

> We crave the sweet: the honey, sugar, kiss
> of berries on our tongue—a happy thought
> to wash the sensors of our brains with bliss
> and push aside the trampled feelings brought
> about by twinges of remorse, regret
> when looking at the empty hive.

Anna West also wrote,

> I want to eat the melancholy I
> can feel inside my ribs, beside my heart.
> I want to eat the sad . . .

I love these lines for their potency and full-on claiming of experience—no standing back opinionating or pontificating. Just a deep dive into sensations of being alive—songs of presence extending in all directions.

Naomi Shihab Nye

There has never been a shortage of hope and change for young artists and writers under the age of twenty-five. It's their currency—to experiment, penetrate layers and realms and eras and elements, participate in many directions, discover what is coming next. Moderation can wait—plenty of time for that later. Now's the time to be an explorer inside the rich hours. When we're lucky enough to risk expressive endeavors, no telling what will happen next. We're rooting for life, stumbling, picking up what we find when we fall.

We never realized how beautiful we were then, a slightly older friend said to me recently, looking through a box of fading pictures. I was stunned to see her at twenty-one, cascading long hair and flowered dress, grinning widely into the camera. We never feel beautiful at all. We feel lumpy, disheveled. And look at us—we were all so beautiful.

One writer I communicated with, Lauren Jensen, wrote that, alas, she had just turned twenty-six, so her poems wouldn't be eligible. She said, "The project sounds, well, cool. I really like the concept of bringing 'young' writers together as at times it feels we should be existing/writing from somewhere we are not. For a few weeks this winter I felt I became a forty-year-old man filled with wit, heartache, and a closet of herringbone . . . I missed my overalls. I missed my hair. And, what was I saying? Maybe just how I like that you're carding at the door, creating a space for young writers to be young, and together . . ."

Carding at the door—made me laugh—come on in, whoever you are. In a time of dire economic downturn and worldwide nervousness about all things financial, writing and reading remain the cheapest arts—and they're portable, too. May your interest continue to exceed your investment.

Whatever age we are, we need to figure out how to keep letting one another into our worlds. What will change? Everything. Better world. Richer fields. Fuller harvest.

Naomi Shihab Nye
San Antonio, Texas

Nicole Guenther

Photons

I said *wouldn't it be amazing*
to be the last bit of light
from a collapsed star?
he said *what?*
I said *wouldn't it be*
amazing? mused
light has to stop
coming at one point
a stream cut off. tilted
back beside him
almost blind walking this dark
road I asked the shadowed sky
wouldn't it be lonely
to be that last light?
he said tentatively *I guess.* still
to the stars I said *I wonder which ones*
have already died. I thought
which stars' last light

like a last breath rushes
towards us now like a final
sigh of air
a final word
unheard and unrecorded.
I said *we might be pulling*
that light into our eyes
this instant. isn't that just
amazing? he looked
at me while I looked
up probing the stars with dreamy
eyes he said
I had never thought
of it that way.
silently I recognized
that as the most
stunning sentence—the most
beautiful words ever uttered.

Experiments in Fire

like our parents always
told us not to like
firefighters warn against
we're playing
games and making
the rules up
as we go we're
matching
warmth to warmth
starting fires burning
wishes into our
skin we're hidden
holding
forbidden lights
we're children
whose fathers have
taught never
touch
but we're finding
these new flames
we smother
at the sound of footsteps

Overlapping

Our atmospheres sift
starlight differently. We filter
different color skies. You mix
my colors. Once primary, I tangle
into purple, orange, green.
Share: give me a tablespoon
of blue and I'll give you a hand
full of yellow, like sunshine
spilled on carpet—purified
by layers, our invisible tropospheres,
mesospheres, stratospheres.
Give me some pink
and I'll laugh and smudge
it on your cheeks. Your ears
will blush. Tap my shoulder,
aim a camera and catch me
mid-smile, oblivious, before I can hold
up my reflexive hand and say, no!
Catch the flash when the shutter
exposes the dark interior
to our radiant lights, the heat
of our colliding thermospheres.

Nicole Guenther

Let me peer out at the world
through your lens. (Maybe I'll shudder,
or gasp, or tilt my head in a question.)
Let me see how your blue
is my turquoise and my orange
is your gold. Suddenly binary
stars, we have startling
gravity. Let's compare
scintillation—let's share
starlight.

6

Membership

I take off my hat on the walk
down to the park
because it feels like a church
and I want my head to feel
connected to the sky, and I realize
it *is* a church—

it contains my religion:
the trees, the birds, the air so smooth
into my lungs. This is my cross,
my prayers, my communion.
I take off my hat because the trees
tell me to. They say, you
walk in a greater world than yourself; show
respect to this powerful world which you
might leave at any time.

I take off my hat
because the creek tells me to, in its silky
constant voice, it says, you are in this church,
you beautiful being, you little person. I take
off my hat and do not speak and say yes
I am a member of this church, I am this small
important nothing, I listen
to the wordless sermon delivered
by you, creek: preacher.

Nicole Guenther

This congregation breathes together
and I take molecules into me,
and carbon dioxide whooshes
out of me, and the plants surrounding
me return my oxygen.

This is why my religion is so
hard to explain. People
say, what do Unitarians
believe? and how can I say, I have faith
in connection and the power I felt
standing on the edge of that cliff
when I was thirteen, and the thunder
of waterfalls, and eye contact,
and words, and changing the world,
and keeping the world the same.

Chase

Berggrun

Question

am I the seventeen I used to be?
my jeans have opened up to clean, thick,
hairy knees

your father is not with us any longer son

what can a white coat do?
warm a
body tempered with
furious anxiety

if my father
asked me
who I am right now
and if I would like
him to come back
I would answer
no
I've come too far

what can the
healthy grass do
to appease the growls
of the lawnmower

do you think . . .

do you think
if you left your house
emily dickinson
your poems would have titles?

shrunk

snaking through the slender grass
i'll cry tears of sugar with the ants

Lauren Espinoza

where I live,

no matter how brown i am—
i'm not brown enough.

Borderlands, Texas.

any Mexican
born on the U.S.
side of the border
can never be considered
a real Mexican
by their brothers who live
across the Rio Grande.

in order to be a real
Mexicano,
i had to come
to the U.S. clandestinely.

i have to have some sort of
"coming over" story.

almost like being
gay and "coming out"
to be legit,
but not quite.

my Spanish may be
grammatically correct,
but if i speak it in
Mexico
too perfect—
What, am i too good
to speak Spanish
to the *señora*
estilo Mexicano?

my Spanish is empty—
like the slaughtered goats
hanging in the market
as i walk through dirt streets
while small dark children follow me
asking if i need a shoeshine or
would like to buy *chicle.*

in the states, i am a wetback;
in Mexico, i am *agringada.*

so what does that make me
when i am in both places at once?

Lauren Espinoza

Borderlands, Texas—

where my home has a U.S. area code,
    but you wouldn't be able to tell it
    by looking at the last names in the phone book.
where every kitchen may not have a loaf of bread,
    but for sure has tortillas.
where you go to the *pulga* to see the movies
    in theaters.
where you don't have to go to the doctor
    to get antibiotics.
where at Macy's, people ask if they can pay in pesos.

throne

i have been to the restroom—
the one labeled Faculty,
where students are not supposed to go.

it has around it an air of prestige
or is it the air
of something more?

there is a couch in the women's
a comfy couch
with southwestern décor.

poor couch,
relegated to live out its life
in the bathroom on the 2nd floor.

maybe it's there so the PhDs
can sit and contemplate;
but, I thought that's what
the commode was for.

either way, i have seen and have sat
on the throne of greatness
where professors go for relief
behind the guard of a closed door.

Lauren Espinoza

death & taxes

when you're dead,
you're done.

when you're a vampire,
you're never done.

when you're working in an office,
you're never done.

vampires have desk jobs,
working at the IRS.

larry does the filing in the basement.
it's so deep underground,

years pass without the undead knowing.
mary sits at her mid-level desk

behind stacks of papers so high
it doesn't matter that there are windows

when you're a vampire in the office
punching the time card with your fangs.

Mackenzie Connellee

window seat 6A

we had been flying for
under an hour when the
turbulence began, rolling
air under the metal
contraption, bouncing
passengers in jerking motions

nothing out the window but
wispy white air, no sign of
land or safety save the
seat cushion flotation device

oh shit, oh shit the boy's
voice behind me muttered,
panicking. I had seen him
in the waiting area, a teenager
with navy sweatshirt sitting
by himself, *I hate flying* he said

I thanked God for the woman
next to him who comforted,
speaking words like *breathe*
and *we're fine* and *don't worry*

but I began to question the
safety of a large metal
bird taking flight, its
wingspan too large to
be completely controlled,
not gliding through air
but using propellers to
press forward, spinning
clouds and atmosphere
backwards into the sky

how much faith does it take
for an airplane to make sense?
too much—now the boy was
speaking in my mind

Mackenzie Connellee

Burkina Faso

it's almost like God
painted in the cracks & crevices,
on roots pinched from the ground.
faces & focuses shift but not for long.
here time moves as a boat sailing over
the smallest river & never laying anchor,
the bicycles swerving with sudden movement.
if you stood in one place forever you might not
see anyone twice, their patterned clothing and
bags of bread. if you wave from a window the people
acknowledge & wave back, searching your face with
their eyes. none of this surfaceness—& how could there
be with so much richness, so much truth? the soil is difficult
to puncture but if you dig deep enough (16 inches down)
you can build a wall with your blistered fingers.
  don't we all
need something to stand on? step in this earth
  and you might find

a reason to stay. look to the Muslim chief
  who stops to help dig the
foundation for a Christian church because
  he has everything to gain.
look to the young boys who walk back and forth
  to the well for sips of
water for workers they don't even know.
  look to all of the people who say
you don't speak my language but that doesn't separate us,
  it's nothing but
a wall to tear down. i don't know you but here is my story—
  a charm for your
necklace; a ring for your finger. take up whatever
  you pull from the dirt & scatter
it somewhere else when nobody is looking.

Mackenzie Connellee

invitation

used to write poetry in art class
when the teacher wasn't looking,
but now i don't take art and i can't
afford not to pay attention in my
classes. now i write poetry in my
free time but that's difficult
because words don't appear like

a dog when you call their name, no,
poetry is anything but convenient.
right now it's 1:05 a.m. because poetry
shook me by the shoulders and said
hey, this is important but now i'm wondering
if the lack of sleep is worth it. i feel
i am always weighing time by the quality
of poems written, because even when

the words grace me with their presence,
they don't always choose to step
delicately into the world, pink shoes
treading softly over the white horizon.
usually poetry slops lazily over the couch
of a page and dangles while i remove its muddy
shoes and rearrange the pillows, all the while
muttering something about Frost and how maybe
his comments against free verse were right
all along (poetry in rhyme always cleans up
after itself) although honestly, you haven't lived
until the homeless free-verse poem on your couch
decides to stay for a cup of tea and, if you're
lucky, lets you take notes on everything he says.

Mackenzie Connellee

suggestion

maybe we try too hard to be
remembered, waking to the
glowing yellow disc in ignorance,
swearing that today will be
the day, today we will make

something of our lives. what
if we are so busy searching
for worth that we miss the
sapphire sky and cackling
blackbird. what else is missing?

maybe our steps are too straight
and our paths too narrow and
not overlapping. maybe when
they overlap someone in another
country lights a candle, a couple

resolves their argument, a young
man puts down his silver gun
and walks away.

Brianne
Carpenter

For My Mom

I praise my mom for blowing the moon off a bridge.
My mom is a fish, swimming in yellow tea.

Eugene Smith

I praise my mother's halle-hallelujah hands
that wind roller sponges up the river
and strings of my hair. She clasps
the sigh of my crayon-colored house and cries
every time she opens the bent paper door.
"Those are the sad eyes of a girl
without a mother," she remembers. Always.
Absence.

     I remember riding the bent springs
of the hospital bed and choosing two
desserts: chocolate pudding and blue jello. I knew
she was getting better because she could taste
the sweet on her tongue and feel my nip
at her toes. Sometimes she was sad
because she couldn't French braid my hair
anymore. Because of my sad eyes. But I pushed
her wheelchair, cut my hair short,
picked up all the beads when they spilled.
I didn't mind.

     As long as I could feel
her palm smooth the creases of my dreams
under covers at night in bed. As long as
she was there.

Plain Stories: Chronology of a Cotton Farmer

I.

I always knew you
were an artifact
he wrote in long
letters he stamped
and sealed and sent
in bottles to her
bedside. She pried open
smooth-tipped pins
and sung them along
the lip-rim of a loose bun
humming, *The world*
is round, the world is
round, my love, the world
will tip you
to me but he lived in
print and seemed to miss
the point of a song
on the tip of a tongue
in the wake of the wind.

Brianne Carpenter

II.

He said, *Birch* and *Baby*
doll, I found you. I had to
get a fingertip dirty, but
I found you.
To which she sang,
I planted a patch
of strawberry seeds. Come, and
kiss these lips and sweet
honey, remember
I'm not your grandmother,
your garden, your patch
of earth. But he tried
anyways. He combed
his fingers up the field
of her back, the bark
of her spine, smoothed
furrows in her hair.
You smell like the damp
ground after a gray storm.
You smell like
rain. So she opened
his hand and gave him
a toy tractor. *Here are*
four wheels for driving with,
if you can ever find
the right width
of road.

III.

The songs she sang she
didn't know the words she
slid on sounds, and
he loved her lyrical.
He bought empty
books to write
her down. He could paw through
pages until the millennium
flipped them back to ashes to
ashes to dust and
regrew them as a tree. She
lived in the ripple
of dune grass, bent
bindings, loosed paper
to sky.

Brianne Carpenter

IV.

She painted
everything green
when she left, and pulled
her sepia face from his
wall. She wanted him
to remember her
in the colors of the forest,
not the brown tones
of a bookstore or
the edges of a teabag, dried.
She laced
her boots for ready, tossed
a petticoat over the table edge
and said, *Here. I guess*
you can eat on this.
He thought the breeze
that blew her
gone
smelled like drought.
And he coughed and
kicked and spat
in the dust, and the spit
seeped the dark sepia
of her face, like a fossil
in the dirt. He always knew
she was bones.

Christmas

Two weeks with my dyed and tongue-pierced sister
  and my dad who plays banjo
rather, who is learning how to pluck and strum
  and forward finger roll
from the woman with the shag–rag mullet sitting
  in a hunter green lawn chair
in front of plastic ficuses that cast blue wall shadows
like the violet stripes of poplar trees on the evening snow
  covering the roof, the road
until our cars become warm frosting knives, glipping across
the surface of a cake, worrying my mom the way
  dinner tables and birthdays do.
My sister asks, honestly, how long do you think until
  he's tired of playing it,
the *t w a n g* she means, the banjo, banjoman in the basement.
He can see himself with the hillbillies in the band
  like he can see himself
with five hundred grand willed to him from the ether, positively
pulled out of the air by a new natural law:
  night dreams, pipe dream principles.
That's just who he is, my mom the stable one
  smoothes over us, nudging
you can love. You can love   the banjoman
buys banjos and paint brushes and golf clubs as she nibbles
  free birthday popcorn

Brianne Carpenter

she bought with dimes. I'll always have to buy
  my own eyeglasses and
my sister, the queen of the monkey bars and mood
swings around us only and who knows why can't we remember
she hates sweet potatoes, school, when you say that,
she wanted to play once too, wanted to fly fine fingers
up and down the chipped keys of the piano my mom
  prayed to us from the ether.

Pupil

One time I saw a *National Geographic*
with eyes on the cover. Eyes
the color of honey and pondwater. Eyes
whose mouth's angle was draped
behind a veil. A whole generation—
that couldn't find Afghanistan
on a map—knew the country by its eyes.
The journalist won prizes.
The child with no more family
left school, was married, made her own.

One time I saw a movie set in 2506,
half a millennium after 1984, but
the government was still keeping track of everyone
by scanning their retinas because
the fingerprint of your eye never changes
—you always have the same soul,
and that never changes either.
It leaps into your eyes when you are born,
which is why you can recognize yourself
in baby pictures, even though you are bald and have no teeth.

Brianne Carpenter

Seventeen years later, *National Geographic*
gathered a search party out of
curiosity, compassion, or because
Afghanistan was important again.
They traveled across oceans and deserts,
through mountains, archives, along the trails
traced by word of mouth
to find eyes.

When they found them, they published an article.
It came with lots of proof and scientific data
because no one could believe that, in seventeen years,
the eyes had found their way
into the worn face of an old woman.
Everyone thought, "She could have been
so beautiful." They thought,
"She could have had a different life."
Some wondered who decides what life is best.
Some gave money.
Many forgot.

If someday, in a morning, you see you,
in a mirror or the dent of a spoon, and wonder
Where is my soul and
Where has it gone, remember this:
Catch the gaze of a woman
on the metro, subway, tram.
Look at a man. Seek and
you will find you
in the slivered space,
a flash between souls. 🔑

43

Brianne Carpenter

Catherine
Bates

The Shooting Range on Mother's Day

It is heat and sweat, the stuff of living
that leads your mother to the shooting range on Mother's Day,
holding metal and fire between her hands.
Your father works on cow fields for some university.
There are test tubes and glass jars filled with animal

parts, paisley-shaped against the glass. Your mama takes
you out to those grassy fields where cow tails swish
back and forth and moo into daybreak.
You will remember your father, treading
over morning grass in between roaming cows,

you are not afraid yet. You believe when your father
starts drinking those Coors Lights it is magic
that makes his eyes a swirly red, the sound of his voice,
lion-pitched and angry, falling into things
as he cries into couch pillows, the palm of your hands,

dinner plates, the open throat of the kitchen sink,
bent-swaggering towards sleep. His cleaning lady
buys him cocaine; her name is Teresa and when
you come over to watch heat lightning
off the back porch your father is already disappearing,

his mind coming apart like pieces to a dandelion,
like the kitchen appliances he has dismantled
because of a soothsayer, because when he burns that cocaine
down into something harder, there are eleven angels

billowing overhead, like a sparkling noose,
like brides guiding him home and it is love
that keeps you waiting at the mouth of the lion,
so on Mother's Day when he comes
over to your mama's house, uninvited

carrying three bottles of Bud Light
in his fingers, part of you knows already
to duck behind the sofa, grip on tight to the leg
of the card table. You can feel the blood moving,
through the star-peeked crevices of your body,

the blood foot stepping through chambers like your father
so many Aprils ago, pressing north through the gated plains,
holding a bucket in the coarse intersection of his hands
as you watch him being taken by the fog,
lost among sleeping cattle and soft brown soil.

Catherine Bates

Through the Barn Doors

In this house of cigarette ash,
where someone is always muttering
a goddamn, jutting elbows into air
like helicopter blades, fighting knuckle
and tooth just to be heard, we are all at it again,

huddled under the night sky like horses, breathing heat
from our nostrils, eyeing the light
underneath the barn door. When someone smashes
through glass or gallops towards
whiskey water, even the dog takes cover.

My sister saunters into her bedroom
salt-lipped and silent, our father pacing
the dark trance of hallways,
then drunk-banging car doors, gunning towards
the fluorescent lights of gas stations and convenience stores
and I am lonely as a hotel room. When the first

bowl is hurled across the dining room table,
the first face slapped, arm grazed, fists
against flesh, our mother is smoking
a slim cigarette outside with the wind chimes
and stray cats, as they walk crooked

into moonlight. Nothing is effortless,
even our dreams fill with carnage,
and when I get the phone call from Dad,
dying again, this time of gangrene,
his leg okra colored and rotten from the hip bone down,
everyone else is just relieved
not to have answered the phone.

Catherine Bates

Paynes Prairie

Arms and legs sprawled like fans under the sun
  were our summers, Lyndsay Bloom swiping a wine cooler
from her mother's six-pack in the fridge, three of us

  around the glassy rim of a fuzzy navel,
drunk off cocoa butter, dark tanning oil:
  How the familiar breath of air-conditioning eased the pain

of our burnt collar bones through summer,
  Lyndsay's older brother thumping on kitchen counters
and tables, winding a beach towel into a whip

  at our forked legs. When the evening broke into night
Mr. Bloom would slide open the porch door and light a joint
  each lawn dimming over with dusk.

When her brother stole the keys to the van
  and said, *hop in*, each of us dove across fur-covered seats,
sun crazed and restless, gold moon swinging through the clouds

like a token for Rocket Mania, the arcade game
　　we played for popcorn and a free large Coke.
Ryan drove the car to Paynes Prairie, fifteen acres of marsh

　　and flatwood pines with the windows rolled down,
seat belts unbuckled, nothing holding us in,
　　three of his friends already out by the dock,

a drink in each of their hands. It was an entirely different
　　game,
　　the high beams flickering on and off from the main road,
the boys somewhere close by, their tiny mouths a strange kind
　　of warmth.

A Lesson on Fire

When the lights grew dim,
the minister struck a match
to the candle of birth.

Maybe I wasn't paying attention
or was watching the Virgin Mary on stage,
eight years old like myself, suffocating

the Cabbage Patch version of baby Jesus
with her armpit, but as the kiss from one candle
to the next spread through the chapel,

my hair fell across the wick,
and like the northern star I gleamed
from the fifth pew down. It was small enough

to put out with your thumb,
but it took my grandmother's fur coat,
my mother's hands, both animal and skin

swatting at my head to put out the flames
caught in my tangled hair. Before the wax
dripped down my sister's wrist,

I felt the marking on my temple,
like a brand on the crest of a cow,
raised and warm. I could smell

the dead parts of me singed,
and was already learning how not to resist,
how to ease into fire, the first of many.

Mary Selph

Fourth or fifth love

I want love to be simple, like
the creased notes you slipped
through locker grates in high school
and as careful as efforts to decipher
what you'd written beneath clouds
of eraser marks. I want the brazenness of poems
stuffed in your backpack when you left
the room. I want us to exist
as we were when the world was still
the bed of your father's truck. I want
to be swallowed whole again
into the whale belly of the sky,
where we'll be churned in dark fluid,
so that if your calloused hands brush
my sweater I'll shiver. If a voice turns
to me, whispers *I love you more*
than life, I'll once again
believe it is I who have
pulled your heart like a heavy plate
from the cabinet of your chest, held it flat
and perfect in my hands
then let go.

Beside a broken-down bus on an overpass outside Philadelphia

"Life is rather raw," she says, clicking
her red fingernails, wondering for a better
word. We're leaning against the guardrail,
watching teenage boys skateboard
below us. The bus driver has given up
looking for answers in the engine
and is smoking a cigarette, talking rapid
Cantonese into his cell phone. She watches how
the boys crash their bodies into the pavement again
and again. Maybe one or two
of them, maybe none of them
will ever be *that good*, and still they crash,
relish the crashing, even, and the moment
of silence when they hover
before plastic wheels smack
the asphalt again. She says
there's something to it—something
like what's in the unshowered bus driver
who spits a wad of tarry mucus
against the dirt then keeps smoking—but something
also like the awe she remembers from childhood

Mary Selph

when a crystal vase smashed against the wall
inches from her skull, and the bits
of glass shattered around her, rainbowing
in the light. Maybe *raw* is the right word.
When she said it, I thought of her biting
into a potato, soil sticking to her lips
as the milky flesh crisped between her teeth. ⚷

My mother decides to seek candidacy as a Methodist minister

I.

My mother practiced silence
in the rigid Sunday morning cathedrals
she grew up in. She stood stiffly each mass
in white stockings and the lace collar
that itched her neck. Alone
before the cross, she steepled her fingers, locked
her knees, and prayed to be holier
than Mary Magdalene and for the courage
to run naked down her street if God asked.

II.

Wednesday evenings my grandparents toted me
like a spare set of keys to a tiny white church
where I sat on oiled wood slab pews
in mended shorts and dust, chanting
Hail Marys, the glass beads pressed between
my fingers. Afterwards, I had my nights
to give monologues to the headstones outside,
to whisper to the dead and to the fireflies.

III.
I know my mother regretted how
she dragged me from one denomination
to the next, regretted the way she sobbed,
falling to her hands and knees in front
of the congregation at the Baptist church,
regretted the solace of the masculine robes,
coarse against her swollen eyes, the palm
curved to her bowed head.

IV.
Later, older, we woke up early one Sunday
morning to drink coffee together
and do laundry. We pulled white sheets fresh
from the wash, toted them outside, pinned them
to the clothesline. It was Christmastime;
I was home from college. There was snow
on the ground, but the sky was a translucent blue,
and the wet sheets soon stiffened with ice.
Half an hour later we shook the crystals free
and brought the sheets inside.

Growing up in woods

When an elder tree collapses,
a younger, suppler one
catches her by the hair before
she hits the ground.

Once, scaling one of the fallen
trees, I reached close enough
to a younger one that her branches gave way
under my added weight, cracking
the old tree's trunk, sending us both down.
We laid then for minutes together, the rotting
wood soft against the snow, still
while the young tree stretched
her limbs at last upward, away.

Mary Selph

Gray
Emerson

The Indexer in Love

Time You Let Me In

65

The Many Secrets of T. S. Eliot

On late nights he would stand
alone in front of his bathroom mirror and
sing "Swanee" loudly, in that old Missouri
drawl he shed to maintain his
poetic image, a stoicism that was
no match for the pleasures
brought to him by
lilacs, Groucho Marx, and
rhyming couplets he would
utter under his breath when
no one was listening,
and once, while drinking,
he confessed that April
was his favorite month
and that he secretly envied
Ezra Pound's moustache.

Ode to Isabella's Hair

Ohhhhhhhhh—the twist of it! The

    Spring!

Sprang!

    Sprung!

Of it! From the frizz-frazz-frazzle curls—

    (the early morning screech of her tangles)

The chit-chat-chattering of dusky locks

    Spun like a starless stretch

Twisting & Twirling

    They're flourishing (ever expanding)

Like the slow quirk of ~~a smile~~ her smile! 🔑

Last Words

I want to go out—
        with a BANG!

No-No-No!

    (Not)—a violent death
    (Not)—a painful death

        a BANG!

(of) words!—
        the best words
            at the best time—in
        the best order

words—relevant
        to the situation
      conscious
        of the imminence
        of My Life's
        consummation

My Words—Spat Out!

with my last breaths

. . . chasing . . . behind

                    My Words—

          (as always)

outrunning

          My Demise 🗝

Gray Emerson

Michelle Brittan

Larry's Produce

My father is at the wheelbarrow
catching persimmons in plastic
bags from my mother's hand.

Here, the jicama learns
to exist with the daikon,
tomatillos and anise make friends.

We dodge a girl with a scepter
of brussels sprouts, and an octogenarian
shows her unwed son how to choose

okra. Citrus and earth mix in the dark air
like Ukrainian and Spanish, *salwar kameez*
and denim—my parents sending me home with

a suitcase's worth of Asian pears.

Fluency

My once-monthly obligation was the phone
like a plastic conch shoved into my young palm, static
ocean carrying my English over eight time zones to Borneo

and reaching this aunt or another with a name
plucked from the Bible, changed
by accent, her laughter not needing
translation as it surfaced. I imagined this

as my mother's revenge for supermarket corrections
on pronunciation, my throat now clotted with the entangled
seaweed of my words made meaningless.
   I can't blame her for the relishing
of my silence. In the end,

I'd flee, the instrument surrendered and her outheld
hand eager to put things back
where they ought to be.

Michelle Brittan

Other Renaissance

When it snows in Tacoma,
the edges of the sky tense like hips
bearing down, and the rain
wants to be something other than it always is.
This kind of cold uncrosses arms
and lifts chins, a shudder that makes palms

open into five-pointed stars
looking to make constellations together.
The wind, pressing into the earth like elbows,
dispels bodies from their houses, pushing
us through the walls and falling onto the streets
of our new lives. As the clouds
whiten like straining knuckles,
the wooden tongues of rooftops catch the first ones
and the city is reinvented,
a white layer of great effort covering us all.

Rootless

Like a net my fingers skim
tap water, cleaning mung bean sprouts
the way you showed me.

    From my palm I find the whole
    ones, fetal curvatures with scalps
    blossoming on tiny yellowed skulls.

    My nail bisects the vertebrae
    from primordial tail, roots
    cast away in the sink.

Though I never learned
the purpose, it's a habit that reminds me
of a time you let me in.

Michelle Brittan

Henry Mills

Tortillas

Your hands teach the flour
    how to make tortillas breathe.

¡Allí mira
    'stan soplando!

You roll the *masa*
    into a ball, a little heart.
Así mira, you show me:
    hug the ball with both palms.
That's the womb isn't it?
    you put yourself inside there.

When I visit the office
    that was once your room
I can still see you
    kneeling by the bed.

¿Abuelita,
    déjame darte un masaje?

I begin, my thumbs
    under your thin white hair,
then down your neck
    where my hands learned
soft circles.

This is the moment
    I don't want to hate my hands
but your arms sag in my palms
    then pale.

This is the moment
    I want to touch you
as if to say thank you,
    but my brown fingers darken
against your translucence.

I want to touch your feet.
    You say no.
When I see them I wonder
    what ate your toes?

I want to ask you,
    was it while you ran with Chambita in your arms
that shrapnel tore his fingers?

Did Abuelito eat
    after he found his daughter facedown in the cobblestone?
What was her name?
    name that appeared among the other names: Rosita,
        Rutilio, Romero?

Henry Mills

In the morning
    did you go out selling tortillas in the aftermath?
Did you chant

        ¡Tortillas!

the same way you chant my name from downstairs?

        ¡Henri!

I hide behind my door.
    I don't respond.
You're coming now.
    Up the steps. Slowly.
You're breathing heavily.
    You're shuffling down the hallway.
You're taking forever.
    I want to scare you.
I want to jump out and startle you.
You're in the doorway.
Your shadow is in my room.
You're almost here.
You're almost here.

For my abuelita, born May 3, 1919, died November 12, 2004

The Torch

When you return to your room
your father is an absence laid
across your bed again,
silent before his *yartzeit* candle.

Downstairs I excavate the office
for some record of him,
instead I find this photograph
of us in the woods.

I'm on your back, the helm—
seat, a blue child-carrier.
I'm chewing my sleeve
wearing a mini pilot's hat.

Your shades are in your shirt pocket;
your Giants baseball cap
is off; the sky is filtered through bramble;
you look proud.

The photographer must be Mom
by the way the shot is focused
on me, clipping the top—
parts of your head outside the frame.

Henry Mills

As the shutter curtain shuts,
you watch Mom glow.
When she puts the camera down
I hope she'll notice your gaze.

This memory has come to me somehow,
although it first must belong to you.
I hear your door lock.
The candle must have died upstairs.

Below me, under the floorboards, wind.
Still the house is quiet.
I sit with this my last star
and inhabit your body.

Run

There is already a helicopter in the sky,
>> a shadow against the stars,
> when my mother steps out of the river,
>>> water rolling off her back.
I've never seen her this way
> nor the way the copilot sees her from the cockpit
>>>> looking down at her body
>>> hot white on his infrared screen.

> Ahead, coyotes have tied tree branches together
>>> to form the tunnel she vanishes into.

This is how my mother is greeted,
>> with a ceremony in the shadows,
> where she ceases to be Salvadoran
>>> and becomes Latina.

There are already agents in the streets
>> when she steps off the bus in Columbia Heights;
>>> already doors kicked in;
>> dogs barking in the wake of men and women
> dragged away, cursing in Spanish;
>>> a pot of bean soup left boiling over
black onto the kitchen floor;
>> men still in their work clothes
>>> on an airplane back to the motherland
> where unforgiving soldiers wait

Henry Mills

to fuck them, torture them,
            tie a lime bag over their heads and fill them with death.

There is already a baby somewhere
                in the back of a crowded hatch,
                        moments from American air.
        This is how I was born,
                turning and kicking through the darkness.
When my mother's eyes met my father's eyes
        there was no common language between them.

    Corre, my mother said to me once, sitting cross-legged on
    her bed.
    Corre, I repeat, and trace the letters in my workbook. ✐

Henry the Horse

I feel like a horse
with a cone tied to its forehead,
talking to a unicorn.
Sometimes I'm too nervous to say, gorgeous,
so I say, great.
You look great in that unicorn outfit.
When really, what I should've said was,
let's run across fields jumping fence after fence
until we collapse,
pressing together our glowing hooves,
you gorgeous beast!
Or maybe I should just take this silly cone off my forehead,
look you in those big unicorn eyes,
lick your snout
and see what happens.

Emily
Hendren

The first Halloween

without window decorations
we noticed, but decided
not to tell you
that it made each of us,
seven and nine, nervous
about being too old
for the black-hatted witches,
gobbly-toothed pumpkins and
purple, hairy, arch-backed cats.
I didn't say a word. Instead
we watched the rain
fall from a place we didn't understand, land heavily
on the tilled and softened grass below.

Yogurt

What kind of Girl Scouts of America sell orange yogurt?
"Orange yogurt! $2.00/cup!" shouts the sign
with the dozen colored pictures
of bouncing, rolling, smiley-faced oranges.
It's not even frozen
yogurt. It is orange, however.
I wonder, *Did they peel all those oranges?*
Was there some badge-earning contest
in a church basement room, thirty-four
eleven-year-olds in orange and brown dresses?
I can see the girl in the middle with her hands on the table,
two braids and gimpish glasses, her chest
quilted in threaded patches and pins.
The smell of orange dyed into her fingertips. Yes,
she, like the Chili's waitress or the barmaid at Diamond's,
she has won.

Emily Hendren

Aragón

We like the air
streaming through our feet
      from fan, or swing set, as if to say
wake up toes!
Wake up little hairs!

      A brush of coolness
on each square
      of skin—
the lingering of one vibrating guitar string—the
"pushing away, making space for" kind
of dance that arrives
      at moments in July.
           (With children

at their hips)
      the women flirt with their shoulders, toss
lightly the breeze feeding
through their blackbrown hair. (The braids even—
      feeling the streams
pass in between each trifold finger.)
The beating
      La jota, la jota! screams
up from tables
and crowds of people waiting
      for their *tinto de verano,*
for their summer dance and salvation.

A recent poem

He sat, waiting,
unsure if the light would stay.
The sun, a gift that day, watched
from the windowsill. His hands,
sweaty, resting in his lap. The blue cloth
of his pants supporting his tired fingers.
Later, he would write about this afternoon,
write it down in some words, some manner
of telling how the breeze softly hummed beneath
the blinds of the office room. Humbly he told them
it was a recent poem, not certain
it would be a last poem.

Inspired by a recording of William Stafford's final reading

Emily Hendren

Lauren Stacks

Evolution of a Writer

One.

When staring out dirty train windows at rows
of brick houses, don't think about the treeless yard, boarded-up
back doors; instead, wonder who lives there and
what time they wake up for
work and what their son's
favorite cartoon is.

Two.

Eavesdrop on strangers and think: I could
use this. "Two blocks is longer than
a driveway," "My cousin is pregnant, but I'm
okay with it," and "You just gotta keep
painting the walls."

Three.

Imagine yourself as someone else. Really
do it. I am my mom. I am
the powdered woman at the grocery
store. I am a dog.

Four.

Brainstorm. Come up with really bad ideas: a poem
for the pet bird you had for three days, a
story about imaginary
friends, an ode to Carly Simon.

Five.

Know that when an idea hits, you will inevitably be
in the wrong place—waiting at a stop light
and searching for a pen, your
eyeliner, anything. For once,
hope the light doesn't turn green
as you scribble nonsense on
your hand, the inside of your wrist. ⚷

Macaroni Love

I say so what if I cry, if my cream
Pillowcase is mascara-stained, if my
Kleenex box is one tissue from being
Empty? What does it matter that water
Squeezes out of the corners of my eyes
Like toothpaste from the bottom of a tube?

You say your main goal is to make me laugh
As much as I cry, to even it all
Out, and I think I like the way that rolls
Off of your tongue, your teeth, like the tears that
Drip off the end of my nose into my
Morning cereal bowl, with elbows like
The curves of macaroni, and now I
Am boiling in hot water, softening.

Rain, Snow, and Other Weather

I'm like the weather, never really can predict
when this rain cloud's gonna
burst; when it's the high or it's
the low, when you might need a light jacket.

Sometimes I'm the slush that sticks
to the bottom of your work pants,
but I can easily be the melting snowflakes
clinging to your long lashes.

I know that some people like:

sunny and seventy-five,
sunny and seventy-five,
sunny and seventy-five,

but you take me as I am and never
forget to pack an umbrella.

You Should Stop Sending

me grad school rejection letters
mixed with birthday cards, utility
bills and my housemate's packages
from god.

stop sending me notes that say *we're
sorry, but* . . . and don't tell me
that i'm good.

all mail needs to stop, flutter
away in the wind, stick in the empty
february branches like leaves that
tell me: *no no no no no*

Jonah
Ogles

Belle Union, Indiana

he still had that drawl that crept slowly,
like speaking molasses. and the day started early
with morning-scrambled eggs and hotcakes so hot
the butter would steam off the top

and he wore faded overalls, covered in pigmud and chickenshit
and the dust from throwing hay bales over the fence,
   where they would land
in quiet clouds of allergens. and he was growing
his first beard, still afraid of college and girls,
of war and German shepherds but still working.
   and not swearing
not smoking or drinking or anything except
   working and dreaming

of something else. something that wasn't farming.
and he dreamed of having sons
   and teaching them to shoot fast and walk quiet and
how to tell that there was a storm coming,
   or that those were red-winged blackbirds
calling from the pasture, and he dreamed that
   they would all go to the woods. to the
mountains. to the dinner table and afterwards
   his sons would wrestle
and argue, and leave red imprints of their hands
   on each other's cheeks.

Time You Let Me In

on Sundays he would wake and go to the Quaker meeting
  in the brick-built
church. the one in the middle of his uncle's cornfield.
  and he would pray.
kneeling in pews, where waiting expectant hands
  had worn through
the finish, and he would wait
for God to speak. and wait
to hear His voice and wait
to lift his eyelid to see
if the girl in the second pew
was looking back. 🗝

Jonah Ogles

on Sunday mornings

I roll out of bed, late
and think of everyone
driving into church on
reckless snow-covered roads.
filing into the sanctuary, starting
to sing along mid-song with
the preacher. saying isn't it
good to be in the house
of the lord. and answering back
it is good.

pulling on ties that
are too tight. sweat rolling
down bald shining faces and
kids crawling under pews
pulling old ladies' pantyhose and
drawing on the attendance
sheet, and reading that
there is no salvation
without grace. amen
hallelujah. thank you.
Jesus

and I am just out of bed, stepping onto
the porch, lighting a cigarette.
thinking that if there is salvation I can't
be redeemed or renewed, but
this morning the sun is shining.
and there are birds. Singing
from these snow-covered trees. 🔑

Jonah Ogles

as far back as I can remember

we've been pissed off,
the whole bloodline, just really pissed.
my great-great-great-grandfather pissed
he left Germany, pissed he picked that
mousy woman to come one month across the ocean with
and two weeks inland, waking up to her every
single day. pissed that she died
and pissed he took that French-Canadian trapper's daughter
who laughed and laughed and never stopped and
maybe that's what drove him to keep the jug
hidden in the shed, behind the oat bags next to
the chair, its legs buried in the dirt and dust
and his anger buried in the whiskey,
passing it on to his children and his grandchildren and their grandchildren
and

my great-grandpa pissed that he lost
the car dealership, and lost the house
and pissed at those goddamned collection men
coming for the car, too.
and pissed, waiting for the kids
to stuff their books into ratty cloth
bags and walk two miles to school
and once they got out of sight
the old man went to find his cigarettes.

and my grandpa had to grow up with the bastard,
pissed as all hell and laughing
cold and mean, and he grew pissed too.
pissed at this goddamn depression,
that they were in the car and without clothes.
pissed and swearing to himself
i'm gonna make
it, goddamn it, i'm
gonna make it

but once he did he was pissed at the pastor
for preaching out of James,
at the fifth for being empty,
at his kids, sliding out left-open windows
running next door and getting stoned
in Jimmy's VW van and laughing
until they cried, and forgetting
to be pissed for a couple of hours

and can you believe it?
we're still pissed

      at God

      at each other

      at mornings

      at late nights

      at the ends of sunsets

      and at rainstorms

and we're still getting together at dinner,
all of us mumbling under our breaths
on the way up the driveway.
still sneaking off for a smoke
and filling the glasses, pissed
at two a.m., but

      we're laughing.

Jesus, you should hear us laugh.

frostbite

my father and I fed cows
at five a.m. our breath
looked like smoke clouds
coming up from a burning field.
our arms moved slow, shoveling
shit into the wheelbarrow.
feed into the pen. my father
sang hymns when his hands
got cold. hymns that I knew,
but didn't sing. he hummed
the verses through his nose.
when he sang the chorus
his breath exploded
into steam.

Jonah Ogles

Emma
Shaw Crane

poem for my name

Been called blanquita
zorrita
güerita
and baby.

Been told I'm most valuable
on my back. Been told I deserved
the slap. Been told I look proper/*you look real nice*
which is WASP for you look real white
and *you looking FINE today girl*
which is code for
you lighter than the friends you with.

Am here to tell you
My name
Emma.
I am
Thick. Gold hoops in my ears.
Afraid to say it out loud but at night I whisper shy
into ink & silence: I poet
Writing myself to life
recording skin stretched warm
over my grandmother's bones
obedience and resistance bound
together in my marrow.

Last night I stood on concrete
iridescent with splinters of glass
like the back of a dead fish
bleeding saltwater blood to newspaper
words swell and slide
no moon
so I wish on the Kool-Aid glow of a neon street lamp
this poem my prayer
for words/clarity/defense

all I got is my name
Emma. Writing myself a
midnight love poem in a broken city.
Recording
simple things:
Gold hoops in my ears. Blood orange
cold and sweet in my hand.
Skin searching warm over
these my bones. ✒

Emma Shaw Crane

kitchen witness

I learned about being a woman in the kitchen
in front of the sink/below a windowsill of glass bluebirds
my grandmother eats standing
after serving my grandfather
he yells over his shoulder for *seconds!*

I learned about being a woman in the kitchen
stirring soup my *tía* tells me
así son los hombres/we gotta work with what we got
at eighteen she bargained out of unprotected rape
memorized his face from her knees
peeling onions I count
the sum of my own narrow escapes
too many
each stinging layer a prayer:
may I never bargain from my knees
may I never trace with ice
the purpled edges of last night's slap

I learned about being a woman in the kitchen
in front of the fridge
my brilliant cousin/hospitalized anorexic at 13
sprays fat-free
I Can't Believe It's Not Butter! onto
low-carb
no-gluten
almost-bread
counting calories the frontline trenches
in her daily battle towards self-elimination

I learned about being a woman in the kitchen
and I'm standing in my kitchen
heartbroken
the haunted expert witness to
my grandmother and her silence
my 82-pound cousin/tubes in her arms
my *tía* on her knees
mouth full of compromise

I stand struggling for breath
facing my inheritance of shame loss & heartbreak
passed through generations like a secret recipe
written across my belly my rib cage my breasts

but the survivor strength of these kitchen stories
got no time for giving up
these women cast-iron strong
5 a.m. light through the open window hopeful
holier than water bread or wine
they whisper
get up off the damn floor
fight back/learn to love
this body
this woman you've become

to answer your questions, reportback beirut

1. *are the young men (rocks in their pockets) jihadis?*
salim yissan shehadi carries
a picture of al-Quds/his cell phone background
loves hip-hop/dabke/the sea
open-palmed offers me mix tapes &
memories: here, the morning my father was shot
here, my seventh birthday without him
here, the uprocking bassline hip-hop heartbeats
my
favorite
song

2. *what did those people say to you?*
do you miss your mother?
habibti come sit beside me/drink
hot sweet tea & kindness
when you go home could you use your english tongue to ask
your people to retract your battleship?

Emma Shaw Crane

3. *why the hell did you go there?*
went looking for words
arnabeet   *al-bahr*   *ya helwe*
cauliflower   the sea   hey beautiful
went running for anything far away
echoes of my arab grandfather's face
waited for me

4. *omg what did you do in the war?*
gunshots roll echo crackback
above us we duck & dive
lay head to head on tile floor below the window
stuck in our apartment for days
sally shi'a/noor sunni/i whitegirl american
we were not meant to practice this fierce collective optimism:
eat labneh
bump palms in the air to fairouz
or braid hair
men in masks shoulder rocket launchers below our balcony
so we talk about the men we love
loss three steps behind anxiety/just
around the corner when your
man is Palestinian in Ein el-Helweh
or darkskinned in America

5. *some crazy shit happens over there!*
thursday, may 22nd, we catch gaza siege
radio from our balcony in beirut. a man calls in
I am bleeding to death
no ambulance/no medic
I want people to know I died this way he says
bleeding out in the dirt/bleeding out without dignity.
he stops
breathing

sunday, may 25th
a text from north oakland
this time, my neighbor's brother
no ambulance/no medic
heartbeats pump blood to concrete
push hope to the gutters
bleeding out bleeding out bleeding out
he stops
breathing

Emma Shaw Crane

6. *baghdad / ramallah / tehran / beirut it's hopeless*
stop. for the sake of our martyrs/killed
crossing *la frontera*/checkpoints/& the intersection of 54th and MLK
buying milk/alone in a cell/bleeding out into cement & dirt
tied to a fence overlooking laramie
stop. & praise
the uprocking bassline hip-hop heartbeats
on my mix tape from salim shehadi
praise lyrical resistance, armed resistance,
& braiding hair/praise
hot sweet tea, the one I love asleep in my bed, praise mothers
praise my *tía* shaking salt & squeezing lime
onto mango with chile pepper saying
baby,
too much work to do
for our oceans of grief
to pull us under

prayer for a soldier back from baghdad

you, my kindergarten best friend come home
talking of nailing breathing targets
drunk/angry you tell me to *SHUT UP*
a lesson I inherited from my grandfather
we a family of marines: the few/the proud
I was three the first time he kicked me
I slammed eyes closed to the rug
rage is a battle scar
semper fi
this is distant war brought home
from Baghdad Okinawa Mosul Tarawa
we the emotional casualties
our childhood of long august afternoons
  n apple branch forts:
collateral damage

what can i ask:
did you shatter Iraqi cheekbones?
did you hang
someone's father from
dislocated shoulders
in the screaming doorways
of Abu Ghraib?

Emma Shaw Crane

at your good-bye barbeque before boot camp
you jumped me into the pool
for a moment in your arms:
before the impact/before the hit
my cheek to your collarbone
my eyes closed against your neck

I repeat this flash second of tenderness like a rosary
my prayer for you/for the rainbow
  you drew me on my seventh birthday
for the people you kill I will never meet
someone else's beloveds:
children blown apart playing marbles
like we used to
under a kitchen table

this my prayer for my grandfather
his angry hands trembling/our relationship sacrificed
for sweaty midnight nightmares of Nagasaki after the bomb
a handful of medals/veterans' bake sales
children that fear him/a black n white photograph
of boy men (the smiling sons of anxious mothers)
  ripped apart
in a war my grandfather will never return from

Time You Let Me In

war takes our men away from us
an invisible   paperless   draft
out of juvenile halls
trailer parks
principals' offices n
single parent poverty

our grandfathers/our cousins/our first loves/
  n our hometown high school kids
come home talking of
nailing   breathing   targets
bring nightmares to our kitchens our orchards
  our bedrooms n our streets

I'm praying in poems for you/my kindergarten best friend
I just want you back alive/I just want you back with your soul
I pray for the people you kill
mothers walking to buy milk
lean gentle young men like you once were
lovers tangled up in each other
children chasing chickens like we used to
n I pray for myself because
what does it mean to love the murderer?

Emma Shaw Crane

Lauren
Eriks

La Belle Dame Sans Merci

I have bed knobs in my hands, portals,
doorways. I can leap over
buildings, baby, bouncing
through walls. I'm free as a
racing rubber ball. When I get lit
on the trail of your Camel cigarette,
you know I can break
every bottle, butt, bombshell around.
I can break free, love, and let
myself go: to pieces, to Bedlam,
to hell, if I like it. I can burn
through lint and linings
of your pockets and roll loose
and untangled, strung out
like laundered lingerie. I won't care
when you say to me: "You look
a mess, child. You look an absolute
mess." I will look beautiful tonight,
and I will not be alone.

My Mother and Merlot:
An Un-Still Life

This was the witching hour:
Your pupils agape, backstroking,
Your irises drenched and drooping,
Weedy with crow-flowers. We once
Thought, as we watched you drown
Away from us, that you had lost
Track of time, outstayed some spell,
Snagged on the drag of the night
And tangled out in a spent spool.

"She has gone," I told my brothers,
"To a white world of wooden sleep,
Where sheets settle like oceans, where
Our ghosts go each day. But she will
See our smiles again, come morning."

And then the night you wove the halls,
Unbuttoned, your smile flapping loose
Like limp laundry. And then I knew:
You were lit like the watery slip
Of the moon, drunk like its shivered
Silver on the jangle of rippled lakes.

Lauren Eriks

When I was a child, you folded fears
Into my belly like kneading
Flour into dough. They swam
On my skin: as I scaled
Pines, as I ran over sea-slicked
Pavement the storm had strewn
With waterlogged earthworms,
As I cried, imagining
Their bodies drawn out like
Shoestrings, sopped and soiled.

I perched on branches, higher
Than houses, and you called me down
From where I drew up
Cracker boxes and house cats
In pulley baskets. That night,
As your watering eyes set sail,
I knew they slipped down
That slogging stream for me.

You said: "You can gather
These moments like worry stones,
Wear them with your palms
To smooth your tree-barked
Ridges, to grow like wax-walled
Pomegranate beads, untasted."

Time You Let Me In

The Color November: Title

for a gray-grained film, an Ang Lee–style
picture, taking place in Montana, spreading out
across blue shale and copper vistas, opening up
with a cowboy—his long arms and the must

of leather—some poor man's
Clint or Kelley, who bends back
the brush, beats bronze trails down
indigo plains, back to a girl, a girl

whose hair—the waves of hay—whose
dress—the soft of sage—whose
winter-wide heart is a horse that pounds
storm, storm, storms into the burnt,

broken bowl of the land.

Lauren Eriks

Sweat Lodge Prayer

Grandmother, give me
The strength of a bear, show me
Your wedding gown watered in white, your eyes
Like Rita Hayworth, your Chicago
Smile, beams like a porch light, like a full
Friday night. I can gasp in your love,
Like your veins, like the blue
Threading roads on the backs of your hands.
I can burn with your breath
As you read me my name. Grandmother,
Give me the strength of a bear.

Jocelyn Stott

A Game of Table Tennis, *In Remembrance*

—For Tina

While my brother and I play Ping-Pong
our pregnant dog, Gypsy, positions

herself under our table, panting with hot
resignation, craving attention that nobody wants

to give. The day's heat and the day's mourning
have caused us all to withdraw and stop

celebrating the coming of new pups.
Sweating with discomfort, she pleads

with bloodshot eyes for relief
from what will be a litter of thirteen.

Cloaked in pain, she belongs
to this scene of grief—her hot breaths

filled with the same ache we won't talk
about while we practice the back

and forth, back and forth, until all the whispered
I just can't believe he's gone's, all the *How tragic*'s,

all the *Oh, his poor family*'s . . . are drowned by her
panting, until all the handkerchiefs and blown

tissues are blotted, too, by the sound
of our game; until my brother has lost

focus and won't look at our dog or at me
or at anything but this ball we keep hitting—forgetting

everything but the ping and the pong of this
pinkish ball, while Gypsy pants

louder and louder—our roughened bare feet
grating hard against Dad's polished deck.

135

Jocelyn Stott

Veteran's Day

I thought you might be my daughter,
he said—his whiskers scratching
the back of my neck, his breath
heating my skin. His hand, cold

from the bottle, dropped mine when I tensed
and it just hung between us like a fish hanging
after its fight to breathe with the hook.
Behind eyes glazed with tears or beer

or just age, he slurs *Everyone's left me.*
So, here in this dark, I let him clench my hand
again; I let him kiss my fingers; and I whisper
how I missed him too. *She was tall,*

he mumbles now—swaying into his words
as if he wants them all back. 🔑

"MADNESS"

it says in red—scrawled perhaps hastily
with your small brush and your trembling hand

or maybe angrily with your fist clenched tight.
It's screaming at me—this word in red:

"MADNESS" is drowning out my tour guide
and I imagine you standing where I stand now

and then marching up in defiance
to this wall that broke a city.

Smothered by my scarf and soaked in this sleet,
the tour group trudges the length of "Death

Strip" to *Checkpoint Charlie*, and I can't escape
your word, my nameless author, your "MADNESS"

telling me of starvation, of shots fired, of 18-year-olds
bleeding at the wall you name "MADNESS." I want

to feel what consumed you the day you committed
your red letters amid the fading, cluttered graffiti.

And I wonder about you and where you hide.
Were you there, my scribe, to see your city divided

Jocelyn Stott

by guards, barbed wire, cement blocks, canines?
Berliner Mauer, your curtain was called. Red-

lettered artist, did you join in '89
all the rioters with hammers and knives? You see

I've become attracted, obsessed—and mad.
I want to touch your vowels and your consonants,

feel the hand that brought them together,
and smell the red paint that introduced us.

When They Came to Re-Tar the Streets

Yesterday, the men in big trucks brought that smell
to my new neighborhood, washing my streets blacker
again. And when my mother visits, she marvels at how
fresh and new and perfect the pitch—I should be proud,

I suppose, of my shiny streets—so I don't tell her
that it bothers me, that it takes me back to our home
when men covered our graying road with tar and stole all
the lines away, painted over the spot where I'd scratched

my name into the black with rocks, burning
my fingers just to finish scraping out my last
letter. Curbside, chin in my knees, I'd trace
the crookedness with my fingers, imagining

the routes of ants that crept below me.
Skin of my elbows ground into that road
just before those men came to cover it all:
the bruises, the stains, the maps I chalked from one

crack to the next—leading to a weed that found
its way through a rip in the road before it smoldered
under the tilt of my glasses, before I invited sun,
with my own lens, into this blackened magic.

Jocelyn Stott

Anna
West

Still Growing

You wake up at 5:23 with dawn
on your sheets and legs as
heavy as if the sun rested
upon them. First you think
you're just a weakling, not used
to walking along the ragged coast for
two hours or through the busy
cobblestone streets. Then
rain, rain, drumbeats under
the bridge, it's too hot, too
cold. So you turn over
in your bed, ignoring the need
to use the toilet, close
your eyes and dream
in Hindi. You are
under the blue sky,
the blue person in the blue
house with the blue couch and
carpet and dishes and sea in
the pictures on the blue walls
and it keeps raining. You
keep raining. You wake up
soaked, but growing requires
moisture and sunlight and
time. 🗝

What It Is

It's your soul that is hungry,
when you wake at night in bed.
You feel the silence of the house,

the air cycling on, off. Alone, you wonder
about dawn, a sunrise you once saw
over the ocean: the sun appeared

from behind a cloud, late into morning,
high above the horizon. You think
of the dogs you once loved who would

prance on sun-washed hardwood floors,
tails wagging as you slid out of bed,
pulled on your robe to take them into the day.

You do not feel like
dancing and there are no
daffodils,

only walls, your bedroom door, and the quiet
of the house, tucked asleep in the night's thick
cover. You wait for dawn. You wait for your

dreams. You wait in the night, and you hunger.

Anna West

Maple Hands in a Wisconsin November, Age 10

She picked that leaf just before she got into the van. The baby
maple tree had been planted by the city yesterday, in the
 narrow
strip of land between the worn cement sidewalk and the
 street.

Tiny green box crisscrossed with gold lines. Encasing two
 leaves,
joined in a **V**, one half the size of the other, both infant. She
 slid
the box into her backpack. Turned around on the bench seat,
 asked

her sister in the back for a book. *Pride and Prejudice.* At the
 hospital,
she clutched the square box in her palm, opened it to tell her
 grandma
about the little tree in the front yard. Her grandma reached
 over

the metal bedrail to hold the narrow stem of the two leaves,
 forcing her
shaking hand out of fist, index finger and thumb finally
 grasping, holding,
dropping those miniature symbols of maple back into the
 box. Later, after

a swim in the hotel pool, water washing over head, under
  back, splashing
from feet and arms, the lines of multicolored flags on the
  ceiling indicating
the nearing pool wall, time to somersault and push off again,
  floating on back,

fingers wrinkled by water, toes wrinkled by water, she placed
her hands on the dry ground along the pool's edge and
  soaking,
hoisted her body out, water dripping, feet leaving watermarks

on cement. Before the week was over, she was shivering in
the cemetery, snowflakes so thick and large, substituting
for tears on the faces of the people walking toward the tent

over the open grave. Her cousin gave her his gloves.

Anna West

Something to Balance

Heath, moor, mountain,
edge of earth
jagged near water,

city streets lined with cars, a bus
driving by, some spire of a cathedral
or church over the row

and underground—
another life—trains, people sitting, standing,
so close to each other that we can choose
what a touch means,
being continually pressed upon

by other accidental hands, leaning
arms reaching for something to balance,
the wind rushing
through the heather, rustling white bells
like a whispering of luck—

and all the while this one house:

white siding, red
brick, small
second story with
a dormer out back

on a tree-lined suburb street,
American, Midwest—

just outside
a dead city
that is more beautiful
than you can imagine, alive
in its broken
colored windowpanes and overgrown
lots—

a curved worn cement
walk leading to the front door:
home.

Anna West

Amal
Khan

Songs of War

A song has murdered the moon
It hangs over my street tonight,
With a texture like sponge.

A sad tune, a wispy old symphony,
a choir of strange, foreign lips.

The song tumbles down the road like a marble
Growing bigger;
Bigger than the men who play it.
Bigger than me.
Bottling my thoughts like pickles
Coughing up my streets, my dust
My precious places
Into spaces. Vast empty spaces.

Now it moves!
So slowly like jazz,
Through a brass tunnel
In old Hollywood
Points two fingers at my eyes
Singing itself to a crest, it dies.

Now, everybody mouths after you,
Those soundless last words.

I see them. They dance out of you—
Coiling extensions of your snake tongue.

Amal Khan

To Be Two

It is a beautiful thing;
This watching from afar.
Wishing for favorable auspices in our hells
And for good weather in the dusty yellow
Of our boundless deserts.
In the convoluted corridors of Otherness,
Passports, surveillance, CCTV,
Your humanity is rejected with the swiftness
Of the final bid of a hand in bridge.

It is, like I have said, a beautiful thing,
To simply be present and observe the orbits
Of your own insides, as you are rotating
Round and round the cavities
Of the most intangible parts of you.
Your soul is flowing and you can see it.
It is a beautiful thing to see, to be Two.

Patience is simply that long lonely stretch of time.
And time is a wise old revolutionary

Promising a Great Paradise, to those who wait.
The skies turn black at the end of every day
But you have turned nowhere special.
And I know because
It is a dark place inside the stars
So it must be a dark place inside you.
A fertile old temple of dreams inside you.

They cannot see the dome, nor the tip of the temple.
They see only the pixels that make you
A pretty spectacle.
An Other. An alien. A biometric border.
They will never recognize
The twos and threes of your soul.

Like the manuals, they will read the binaries;
The zero, the one, the zero, the one.
To them, there is no more to you.
Than the zero, the one, the zero, the one.

Amal Khan

Summer Aches

Yellow droplets have fallen to the city
From the only sky a leaf has ever known.

In my mother's garden, stands one such tree
Gifting her daughter its strange name.

But the *Amal-taas* outside is still bare.
"Wait," Ami says, *"ours always blooms last."*

Listen with Care

Certainly in the core, the very heart of the plum.
Beneath the flavor of its golden hairs
There is language.
I am certain . . . this is certain
It is almost certainly there.

There is, at least, some comfort in the habits
Of the earth.
In the customs of nature, I found the sun.
And all the heart's languages in the crease of a plum.

They have called me subcontinental,
Ethnic and oriental—
Suffering and my creed—
It is a romantic thing indeed.

But even history is bored with the repetition
Of death. Upon death. Upon rose-colored death.

Newsweek said my Pakistan is now
The most dangerous place on earth.
This substantially increases my rhetorical worth.

Amal Khan

4 a.m.

Long distance. Phone card. PIN number. Country code.
The buttons . . . have they always been this size?
My hands are trembling. I dial three times.
Wars spilling into my streets every day,
I swear there is nothing poetic in this.
In the fear.
In asking,
Ama, is everyone okay?

So forgive me, friend, when I wake the next morning
And walk my way a little quietly around life
And the lunch table.
Forgive me when I have no strength to explain
Matters of the soul.
This helplessness, friend, it has taken me whole.

Yet I have learned.
In chronicles of sorrow, too, there are joys,
In lesions of silence, immeasurable noise.
And certainly in the very pit of the heart
Beneath the trouble in the valves
There is kindness.
Certainly in the ruby heart of this plum's seasons,
A silent reason for hope.

Margaret Bashaar

Living with a Bodhisattva Cat Is Intimidating

The Bodhisattva Cat is, of course, vegan:
He will not eat the inexpensive dry food
   I fed my last cat, who was unenlightened.

He is morally opposed to hunting,
compassionately watches moles skitter
   across the basement floor.

The Bodhisattava Cat meditates for up to eighteen hours
   a day,
gives impromptu dharma talks to squirrels perched
   on the bird feeder outside my kitchen window.

The Bodhisattva Cat has boycotted the 2008 Olympics
   in Beijing:
I read about the torch relay on Yahoo! News
   and he looked at his paws.

He destroys all my knitting to teach me
   about impermanence.

To My Lover, Who Tells Me He Is Old

I have never climbed
the wall of an ashram, served food
in white linen, head shaved and bowed,
and yes,
we both know the smell
of honeysuckle from our mothers
or grandmothers, we have both
been stitched back together.
But you tell me your father
held you with no anesthetic,
that you were praised
when you did not cry out, and I remember
how my whole body shook yesterday
at the burn of Novocain and the mute tug
of sutures in my chin.
I lay on a hospital stretcher and clutched
the hand of a doctor
who claimed he could tell
I am in love, that all Romanian brides
wear combat boots under their wedding dresses,
and as he sewed up my skin I thought
of Sunday mornings and how I am
always thankful I can comb your hair
away from your face and count
a gray one for each finger.

Margaret Bashaar

My Summer with the Norseman

The Viking and I never spoke
the same language. He picked me up
off the shore of a sick green ocean,
took me to his mud–brick home
and pushed two straw pallets together,
smiled hopefully.

He believed that he had saved me
from wars and storm foam,
gray afternoons
spent fishing for skate egg sacs.

For ten weeks
I let him bring me salted meat
and white silk corsets,
speak to me in soft, guttural tones
when I smiled. On warm days
he would walk with me
through his village, gesture to the women
who were with child
by mates they could not understand,
make me presents
of wilted wild flowers
held out in his pale, meaty fist.

He had no horned helmet or longboat,
only a silver ear-spoon and a leather pouch
full of smooth, gray stones he cast into a circle
while I pretended to sleep.

As August ended and cold wind
blew in from the northern shore
I ran down to the ocean,
snail shells and rocks cutting my feet.
I stood ankle-deep in the surf,
waited for the sea-gods to save me,
and the Viking filled his hut
with dead flowers.

Margaret Bashaar

Severe

April doesn't drink anymore—bottles
of gin and vodka collect dust
beneath her sink, caps rusted in place.
The light in the bathroom burns her eyes.
The hot water knob is broken.

She listens to commercials
on the radio and changes the station
when music comes on. It's been three months
since she slept without dreaming
about empty, windowless rooms that stink
of midsummer compost.

She boils water for tea
but always forgets to add the bag,
boils the same pot
morning and evening,
hands gray with cold.
Now there are circles like bruises
around her eyes and she says,
I only fall in love
with fictional men these days.
They never tangle my rib cage.

Tala
Abu Rahmeh

Upon Arrival

I don't know anymore,
What if I love it more, over there?
What's not to love over here?

Mama says there is nothing like home
Everyone knows you and even if they don't
They still impose.

I used to say take me home
Where everybody can pronounce my name,
Roll it off of the tongue like sugar, take me

Home.

I shake hands of relatives
I never liked
"Yes, of course I will come back to the country,

If we, the educated, don't come back
Who will?"
I want to scream:

I'm getting too used to having
A dignity. I'm getting used to not crossing
Checkpoints, I'm getting used to staying out
Late without the fear of a tank barging in, I'm getting

used to crying, over little things, like if the bus is late,
or the milk has run out.

Tala Abu Rahmeh

Comfort Poem

to Keith Leonard

I.
I think about light a lot. Remember
a day when you ate a burrito with a fork,
played with its edges while I picked
my heart apart.

"It's good to be needed," you said and my eyes welled.
A sun the size of a spotlight leaked from the window,
and your hands spread warmth.

There is much hope in syllables,
but a giant love in whatever remains
unsaid.

II.
Loving you is easy, and at a time when nightmares
occupy my sleep, it's necessary.

Every time I dream of her, she is dying,
once on a plastic bed, the next on the steps of a church.
Everyone thinks out loud:
"Maybe she'll live." Except for me.

You put your hands inside mine,
"We know sorrow's thick ankles," you say.
During the inch of silence, before I cry,
I see many bright mornings, coming your way.

I walk away into a world
of concrete wilderness,
but even the metallic rectangles of barbed wire know
a mama, like mine, lived in all different directions.

III.
Cancer is like a needle.
Life in its eye; death on its tip.
A lesion, the size of Rome, stretches in my chest.

Tala Abu Rahmeh

The Falling Man [and every person who jumped from the twin towers as they fell to the ground]

You walk, like an open wound, your heart peeking from the skin, swallowing the pain of the city. He is in every curve of your face. As life becomes ordinary for passersby you want to scream, "I am his mother. I am his mother and he died and I saw him twirl and curl into a thud. I am his mother and I know all of his limbs, the scars, the edges of his knees and heart and I saw him twirl and curl into a thud. I am his mother and I feel bits of him left in my uterus, they pinch me from the inside when I'm about to forget and I saw him twirl and curl into a thud. I am his mother and I kissed his eyelashes when he told me he wanted to be ordinary and I saw him twirl and curl into a thud. I am his mother and I know how his eyes tighten and fingers bend when he laughs and I saw him twirl and curl into a thud. I am his mother and I taught him how to love with reservation so not to get his heart broken but he never listened and I saw him twirl and curl into a thud. I am his mother and I know that when he eats he chews slowly to protect his teeth from decay and I saw him twirl and curl into a thud. I am his mother and I watched him cross the street for the first time and I saw him twirl and curl into a thud. I am his mother and when I dream of him I see him standing."

I Hear Quran

The prayers are braided.
The small reader
annunciates Words
made of honey. But I
feel stuck, at a funeral.
God sits on my mother's chest.
His face is her pendant,
golden with a slight hint
of decay. A friend says I sound
like a perfect Catholic,
except for this whole
worshipping Jesus part.
I'm stranded. I wait
for one label to glue
on my forehead, but I think
God forgot my address?
I want His hands, to cup
my heart. I want Him
to seal it away
from numbness.
But I know He has more
important things to do: knit
mosquito nets
and make sure that at least
the dead are equal.

Tala Abu Rahmeh

Kayla
Sargeson

Thanksgiving Wishes for My Grandfather
in memory of Robert Brashears

It's grayer here in this mill town
by the Ohio than it is in the city.
You'd hate it there, where the traffic lights
and hospitals light up the sky.
You'd favor the way the mill brightens the sky here
in Monaca, Pennsylvania.

Thursday, we have our first Thanksgiving without you.
After Grammy goes to bed,
I have a cigarette outside.
I think I can see death standing in the snow-filled alley
behind our house.
The cigarette makes my chest feel tight and I wonder
if this is how you felt when you were dying,
if you felt it coming a long time before it did,
or did you just fade away?
I leave the bathroom light on after I go upstairs
like I did when you were alive.

To My Grandfather, a Year Later

It's 3:00 p.m. on February 18, 2008.
You've been dead exactly a year.
It feels like longer.

I'm writing to your soul
because your body is ashes,
hidden away in an urn somewhere in the house.
(Mom and Grammy can't agree on where to bury you.
Grammy says the mountains like you wanted.
Mom just cries.)
I'm writing to tell you
Mom won't leave Andy
even though he quit speaking to Hannah,
who finally took her SATs and applied to Carlow.
She's not dating that loser Timmy anymore.
Grammy's fine.
She goes gambling from time to time.
Your death gave her freedom.
She loves you for it.
I quit speaking to the boy I was sleeping with
you didn't know about.
Kyle and I are long since over.
I made the dean's list.
I'm going to be published in the spring, and
I'm moving into an apartment next year.

Kayla Sargeson

I'm writing mostly to thank you for living
your eighty years
and to tell you I love you
and think of you often.

To My Rapist, after a Tour of the Lower Ninth Ward of New Orleans

Dog not found written on one of the houses
God Lives on another.
Well, I can't find God anywhere down here,
where *DOA* is still painted on the exterior
of some of the houses.
Then again, I'm not looking hard to find
Him, or Her, or Whoever God may be.
I'm not sure what I'm looking for here, really, but
I end up finding the strength
that comes from the people of New Orleans,
with their slow *y'alls*
and their plates of spicy jambalaya and steamy corn bread.
Their welcoming smiles, *darlin's*
fried crawfish, messy po'boys,
bright French Quarter, smooth jazz
becomes what saves me.
Only the strong survive natural disasters.
Rape isn't natural, but it is a disaster.
Well, maybe it is natural, like rain
like hurricanes, levees breaking.
Like with New Orleans, people don't understand
  what happened to me
and my friends don't want to talk about it anymore.
Get over it, their eyes say
the way Northerners say, *don't rebuild.*
New Orleans is a disaster. It will just get ruined again.

Kayla Sargeson

Getting over what you did to me is not why
I get out of bed anymore.

The Happiest Moment of My Life Was When I Realized I Was Happy

I'm brought back in the Louisiana breeze,
wet paint glittering through the sunlight,
laughter of New Orleans children,
teaching us dances to songs like:
Let it rain / now wash it out.

When we stare dumbly, they say:
*What do you mean Pittsburgh doesn't have
the Chicken Noodle dance?*

I love them,
the children whose homes are FEMA trailers bordering
the wreckage of their once houses—
Over and over they thank us,
like my group and I were misfit angels
with paint on our clothes and in our hair,
mud covering the bottoms of our shoes.

Kayla Sargeson

Ben
Westlie

And there are Ghosts

At night
        you can hear them,
              talking
                    about when
they were alive, when it was them
        sleeping
              in the room you now lie down in,

shut your eyes in,
to depart yourself for just a few hours.
        Sometimes they sound angry
                  causing pipes to shout and floors
to creak and you
      can't help but hear
               breathing which you tell yourself
is just air finding
      the cracks in
              the window frame. Why shouldn't they
display such bitterness, you're the body, the

life, the memory, you get to still
feel, you
have the time they envy. You hold
tighter to the warmth that is your
shield.
You hope the furnace will
stop making footstep sounds outside
your door,
silently call for sleep
to seduce you, but most of all you
try to be
very happy, if they
do enter your room, it is the very
heat your body
releases when
you feel joy that they glide into,
becoming undead.

The Groom's Man

You never taught me how to be happy for you
on your wedding day.
You're someone I don't know now,

someone I have not yet learned to love.
You never told me I would be jealous,
how much I would fear you would leave our friendship behind
like a city you once lived in.
You show me your white dress with pearl sequins,
I want to be one of those sequins, near to you, glossy,
a tiny, round dawn.

Looking at Her Canvases

She collages her disasters
by finding her own feelings in the
magazine faces.
The magazines do not have the same need.

Painted-on colors
burst from eyes, mouths, curves
beckoning
for some substance of truth,

more than the pills
with similar colors dissolving in her,
their chemicals racing to the brain
in a questionable rescue.

The glue, the glitter, the fabric:
She chooses where each particle
should go on canvas, the placement
makes her less a floating grief

Ben Westlie

colliding with the rest
of us roaming fossils.

Sometimes there are words
among the images
when the images are not enough.
She slips in and out of them,
incognito.

Finding Our Flag

We were just boys acting like
superheroes in the woods
when we came upon it,
the red and the white stripes torn, and
bleached by the sun.

The stars, fewer than fifty
and with blurred shapes like explosions.
We knew what it was in school,
we sang to it as our right hands sheltered our hearts.
But never had we seen the flag like this.

We picked the flag up and wrapped it around our shoulders like
a native shawl,
we put it around our heads like a shaman's turban,
we let it hang from our brows like a nun's veil,
we put it around our hips and pranced around in a girlish
dance, out of ourselves.

Ben Westlie

My friend froze.
Someone died fighting for this flag, he said.
Then my friend threw the flag to the ground,
put his head right over my heart,
while my arms, possessed, found their way around his torso.

Boys were not supposed to hug this long
or ever.
Because of this torn, disfigured, sun-bleached flag
we were boys who would be men,
embracing each other, crying.

Matthew
Baker

foundling

most of you are unaware that i was adopted by the people i now call my parents when i was six years old. my parents were visiting a seatown, staying in a tiny cottage near the fish market, when they found me living underneath a dock with wharf rats and rag pickers, naked and wild. i threw rocks at them and they fell in love with me. so they baited me from the docks to the airstrip with cheap trinkets, thimbles and copper coins, and carried me onto an airplane, feeding me cookies to keep me quiet. only vaguely do i remember any of this. my memories of my orphan life are mismatched and blurred, like someone held them underwater while they were still wet and everything smeared. my parents never talk about the abduction, probably hoping that i have forgotten. and of course they never told my sisters. i am only telling you this because if we have trouble understanding each other, i want you to know that it is because my people are different from your own. your people are my parents' people, gray television eyes, coffee-stained teeth. your people speak grocery store magazine. your people are golfers. my people, we are aliens, we have dark whale eyes and our hair clumps like seaweed and we speak four languages you cannot understand. we are always in our barefeet. we are nomads, sleeping on boats, forgetting our children under the docks. we steal vegetable seeds. we have milkteeth and hollow bird bones and we hunt imaginary things, ghost elk, mewl bats, mock turtles, roasting them over beachfires. we are nocturnal, drinking calabashes of cider, translating color into mandolin strings. we are an endangered species, tree scramblers, wind eaters, we are orphans, all of us, trying to blend in with the rest of you, trying to pretend that we aren't afraid of anything.

195

sidewalk chalk

i am still waiting for my seventh birthday,
for skinny calves and rib skin, for candles

i can fit into a single breath, for hands
that are fingers growing from wrists,

for watermelon seeds to grow gardens
in my stomach, for words to taste like

cartoon bubbles, for green socks to be
another sort of adventure, for a crowded

street full of umbrellas to become
a sea of trampolines, for dinosaurs

to loom larger than death,
for a washing machine to be the monster

in my basement, for winter jackets to be
the monster in my closet, for emptiness

to be the monster under my bed, waiting
for me while i sleep, tangled in sheets,

while i dream, while i pray, while i wait for
birthday balloons that hang helium high

and brush the ceiling, bobbing back and forth
like rubber cobras charmed from the depths

of whatever basket must be inside
my mother's chest, those brittle reeds

expanding to hold her hostage breath,
that basket she built in my father's

absence, like the way a bird can
sometimes swallow the horizon whole.

Matthew Baker

ode to poetry

i spit on you, poetry. this is me spitting on you. this is me
egging your cocker spaniel. this is me stomping
your children's halloween pumpkins. you are
dead to me, poetry. i was only using you for the sex.
i never loved you. you are overweight.
this is me spitting on you. this is me
outside your bedroom window with torches,
with all of the neighbors, chanting.
we are coming for you. we are rustling
in the alleys, we are leaning against the bus stops,
we are sitting in the shadows of garbage cans, we are
dragging Shakespeare out of the local tavern and
under the streetlights and beating him to death
with empty bottles. we are coming for you.

you cannot stop us. you are old and frail and
unwanted. we are dragging Whitman
out of his cabin, carrying him
into the trees and the moonlight,
dragging him into the creek, shoving him
under the water, watching him thrash, listening to
the crickets. we are everywhere. we are insomnia.
we are burning your fields, we are swarming
your monuments, we are executing Yeats, Rilke, Dr. Seuss,
dangling their bodies from flagpoles. we are
watching you from the rooftops. you cannot stop us.
you are nothing, poetry. you are the weak, the helpless,
the unevolved. you are the entire state of delaware
yawning in unison. you are rhyming, no one cares.

dying man on a hospital bed

the sparrows have come
again. they are
perched on

the powerlines. i am
still breathing. the sky
is blue. there are no

clouds. the nurse
has forgotten to bring
me more mustard.

Allison
Rivers

Even Before You

In the month I was alive
before you were born,
the geese flew overhead in a crooked line.
My mother made hot chocolate
without marshmallows.

Turning Seven in the Pediatrics Unit

We're going to give you a bracelet
the doctor said,
a plastic, yellow, holy thing.
"Happy Birthday," he said as it
snapped onto my wrist.
They stretched me down the hall.
Ivy wrapped around my arm,
wove into the inside of my elbow.
Screens beeped like robots.
They called me broken
like my sister's doll, like
the cookie I dropped this morning
on the kitchen floor.
They made a hole in my chest
where God looked in
and saw my heart.
Will He still love me
if I fail the test? When
they find the demon in my tummy?
He cannot hug me
tight like this blood pressure cuff.

Allison Rivers

The Giving Tree

for my father

You read to me.
The Giving Tree, always.
I sat on your lap in that blue room.
The walls were blank.
You taught me how to hold
a golf club, and
we chipped imagined shots
onto the bed. You
made us spaghetti
and you drank
red wine. The plates
were painted with pictures
of the countryside.
You punched numbers into
the microwave using your
middle finger, and
I wondered if you knew
that wasn't nice.
We watched golf on TV
and ate popcorn,
losing pieces in
the crevices of the recliner.

I never did understand
why the tree was still happy
at the end. The little boy
used her until she was
nothing but a stump.
She couldn't even run away.
But the ending was always the same:
"And the tree was happy."

At night I cried,
crawled behind the bed,
and made collect calls
to my mother.

Allison Rivers

The Dead Woman Left Her Signature
in the Front of My Book, or What I Have Left
for John & Julie Rybicki

There's a dead woman's handwriting
on my poems. She sat in front of me
before she died, told me she wanted more
to the story. Her husband stroked her arm.
He looked at her like he was hanging onto
a kite whose string he knew,
they both knew,
would snap right above his white-knuckled reach.

Before my mother left on a business trip,
she gave me a piece of gum.
I chewed it for three days,
let it fall apart in my mouth,
convinced it would be the only thing I had left.

Laura Lee
Beasley

Double Elegy

For their fiftieth wedding anniversary
my grandparents took a South American cruise.
They planned for months, buying guides
to each port of call, Punta Arenas, Esmeraldas,
packing and unpacking their suitcases,
folding in Bermuda shorts and disposable cameras,
to capture the rain forests' orchids,
the giant leaf-cutter ants and red-eyed tree frogs.
At a specialty shop they purchased hanging pouches
to hide their wallets from pickpockets,
compact umbrellas the size of playing cards.

I like to imagine them in their stateroom,
before the dinner service, with sunburnt noses,
having spent all day stumbling through
crowded markets full of papayas, bananas,
and stray dogs, trekking down trails
of tangled vines to find some cold waterfall,
my grandfather in his one wrinkled suit,
my grandmother in a navy evening gown,
a whole buffet of lobster tails, rock shrimp,
and champagne flutes waiting for them,
so many stops still left on the itinerary.

Leaving

Leaving the hospital we stop for burgers
near the interstate entrance ramp.
We eat without talking in the shadowed car,
then my brother says, *She'll be ok.*
He looks ridiculous, ketchup and mustard
dripping down the sides of his face.
We turn onto the darkening highway.
I don't say anything,
but I know she is still there,
her arms, pale and folded across her chest,
and her sheets, folds of them covering her body.
Like flowers, reversed in time-lapse photography,
I know they will keep folding,
all that white folding into white,
the blossoms turning back to buds,
the petals tightening, until one day
there will be nothing—
just a neatly made hospital bed,
and this flat line of highway before us.

Laura Lee Beasley

Nothing

Even when we were young it rested beneath
the floorboards, stirring at the sounds of footsteps.
We crawled to feed it pennies and Cheerios
through the slits of an air-conditioning vent.
And there were other places we found it too.
At the pier on Saint Simon's Island,
covered with sunlight and the smell of fish guts,
it shifted beneath the waves, gulping
up our lures into its great darkness.
Sometimes it lay curled in the post office box
at the end of our street like a cat sleeping,
soft and purring, waiting for the mail.
Once instead of the mail we fed it a robin's egg,
stolen from the birdhouse in our backyard,
with a blue shell still warm from the nest.
It was there all our lives, in the backs of closets,
in the shadowed woods behind the playground,
in our bedrooms at night, watching us sleep.
But somehow we were still shocked by it
when we sat at our grandmother's bedside
holding her hands as it pulled her in, into
its widening mouth, a snake swallowing a mouse.

The Egyptians

The Egyptians dipped the hands
of their dead in gold,
so that neither death nor salt
could shrivel the fingers.
They pulled out the organs,
heavy as balls of bread dough,
and encased them in jade.
They built toy-sized ships,
decked with full wooden crews,
to become real in the afterlife.
So how could I have only
eaten the leftovers in your fridge,
boxed up your collection
of paperback murder mysteries,
wrapped myself in your faded green coat?

Laura Lee Beasley

Mario
Chard

Sacrament

She spoke to us
      the way she spoke with apparitions
in the garden.
      Said she learned enough of telling lies
though I alone
      believed her. How in the dark rows

      of raspberries,
          she would call to them, *perdóname*,
then each night
      rinse her hands for dinner, a gardener's
only sacrament.
      She who knew water for more than thirst,

who could not
      find the line between the water turning
dark and her dark
      hands, what could she trust but *lorem ipsum*?
Buried seeds waiting
      for the true leaves to follow?

Noticing the Lesion

I would tell you of my father's arm
but I would tell you first of peaches,

and the orchard that my father built
of peaches, and how its order goes

unnoticed from the roadway, the rows
of trees appear as rows until you step

aside that pattern for the peach you lost
while gathering, and all the structured lanes

become as knots, and all the rush of order
quakes beneath you, but the fallen peach

you hold, rotting where it fell, its violet bruise
a pattern of a planet and its satellite,

some line of weight between them broken,
would tell you more perhaps of lesions

than any son who watched his father
quickly pull his sleeve down to his wrist.

Mario Chard

On the Question of What Drives Coronary Circulation, Biology Class, Morgan High School, 1999

Because it seemed sensible then
to ask, considering the compounds
we discussed, how process coursed
on to further process as curtains parting
backward, I took his silence as a sign
of reflection. Then Mr. Mowery,

with all the steady grace of a man
who knew the sacrifice of his responses,
who must have regretted the analogy
of the body's inner workings to a city's
infrastructure, decided instead to answer
with his eyes, the first true look
he ever gave directly, leaving me
to wonder how he could have sensed
the deeper inquiry of a student
who only questioned the function
of arteries, one who learned too late,

perhaps, while mapping the bloodlines
back to the drum of their source,
that every new study of the body
must lead to this same fear, sustained
by the memory I then recalled of a night
preceding Christmas, my mother alone
in the living room, dressing the tree
she redeemed from a box in the corner,
and I who could not sleep beside her,
watching her restore the order
of branches and needles, threading
its limbs with tubes and colored lanterns,
bulbs of light and streaming fluid,
so that I turned, startled by that illumination,
held her side until the rushing of those lights
had ceased and I could fall asleep. ✎

Mario Chard

To Know the Difference

You must run this mountain without pause.
In the evening or the afternoon,
you must cross the first fields waking
to your footsteps, stormwashed at the foothills.

In the evening or the afternoon, in the closing
of a shadowline, you must read aloud
the reddened last words of this canyon's leaves
to the trees that clap their hands.

NOTES ON THE CONTRIBUTORS

In school I was good with words and bad with numbers—that's why there are 26 poets in this book, not 25. I loved them all and could hardly omit anyone after writing all the poets cheerily to say their poems were accepted! I would rather embrace my flaws.

—N.S.N.

 Matthew Baker got into a fight on the school bus in third grade and was almost suspended. In fourth grade he fought on the playground and was nearly suspended again. After that things settled down. During a homeless period, he slept in a dugout at a stadium, behind some pianos at a local theater, and on the porch of an abandoned house near a beach.

 Margaret Bashaar does much of her writing on a typewriter named Frida which she found abandoned in a park. A Bon Buddhist, she is obsessed with Dada. She is still a little bit afraid of the dark.

 Catherine Bates is a perpetual procrastinator and a sincere pessimist. Terrible at math, she loves gardenias, the scent of marshmallows still in the bag, and the sounds of her sleeping dog. She appreciates the feeling of holding a book in her hands and has a secret affinity for astrology.

 Laura Lee Beasley could be related to anyone since her grandmother was left on her great-grandmother's doorstep one night during the Great Depression. As a child she tortured her little brother by convincing him he was turning into a squirrel. The first book she read was *Little House in the Big Woods*, and her first leading role in a play was as Laura Ingalls Wilder. She would have beautiful pictures of her trip to Paris if only she knew how to properly load a camera with film. *www.lauraleebeasley.com*

Chase Berggrun learned to read when he was three years old. He now owns twelve antique typewriters, which he uses exclusively to draft his writing. His favorite is a Royal Portable named Lenin. An unabashed Russophile, he has an entire bookshelf filled with Tolstoy, Mayakovsky, Nabokov, and Mandelshtam. He spends too much money (whenever he has it) on books, and far too little on food. He's also obsessed with the Spanish Civil War and foreign poets (Neruda, Rilke, Agha Shahid Ali, etc.). He has frequently been ejected from history classes for anarchist outbursts. He never sleeps.

Michelle Brittan, our title poet, was born in San Francisco of mixed white and Malaysian heritage. She knows many great details about Fresno, California, including where the best peach ice cream is. *michellebrittan.wordpress.com*

Brianne Carpenter knows next to nothing about pop culture. She once asked if Rambo was a clown. She loves poetry read aloud and miniature kitchen utensils. Her collection includes a heart-shaped egg mold, eight mini ramekins, and a tiny spatula. *briannecarpenter.wordpress.com*

Mario Chard would like to work as a chauffeur by day and a poet by night. He took his future wife to a Don McLean concert for their first date, and once slept in a hammock on a cliff overlooking the ocean in Puerto Rico. As a child he spoke Spanish and English ("I have always lived with my blood divided") and used to request travel brochures from all over the country. He always keeps a copy of Philip Levine's poem "M. Degas Teaches Art & Science at Durfee Intermediate School—Detroit, 1942" in his pocket. *web.ics.purdue.edu/~mchard*

Mackenzie Connellee loves chai tea lattes and Jesus Christ. Her favorite clothing is a pair of navy rain boots with Dalmatians painted on the sides. She loves playing tennis and going on adventures with her sister and best friend, Morgan.

Emma Shaw Crane met her first love in high school detention. Her favorite taste is mango with lime, salt, and chili pepper. She grew up on an apple farm near a small, dusty agricultural town and also lived in Mexico as a child. Her most ecstatic recent moment was when she discovered her mother secretly writes poetry in a little notebook she keeps in the glove compartment of her car. She has studied Arabic in Lebanon and believes poetry is "a way of telling the truth and an expression of human dignity."

Gray Emerson claims to have "more faults than merits"—late nights, fast food, rants, and spending more money than he has. He enjoys comic books, film noir, Brazilian music, and cartoons. He counts Frank Capra, Wallace Stevens, Cole Porter, and e. e. cummings as influences. His favorite book is *The Maltese Falcon*.

Lauren Eriks has studied in France, Austria, and England, as well as in the United States. She hopes to spend the next half decade earning poverty wages in exotic places. She's an avid backpacker, a photography enthusiast, and a connoisseur of epic films of questionable quality. In eighth grade she wrote the first two hundred pages of a fantasy/ sci-fi novel, whose conclusion is (in all likelihood permanently) forthcoming. *laureneriks.wordpress.com*

Lauren Espinoza is an only child who has been living in the same room in the same home in the Rio Grande Valley since she was born. When not going to school or working, she can be found on her computer, in bed, or playing with the puppy that burrows into her sheets with his tiny wet nose. She could eat her weight in spaghetti. *lauren-out-loud.blogspot.com*

 Nicole Guenther is an autodidactic vegetarian feminist babysitting Unitarian homeschooler who has read more than 1,207 books since September 2002. She adores babies. Her writing submissions have an overall acceptance rate of 4.4%. Because of poetry, she no longer has any qualms about rejection.

 Emily Hendren loves fresh flowers and the idea of bringing them home to sit in a glass, though she always forgets to water them. Her favorite piece of clothing is a mustard-colored scarf from Ireland. In her life, she likes to think she has *almost* done lots of things—*almost* been a concert pianist, an Olympic gymnast, and an accomplished skier. She has started and stopped reading *The Brothers Karamazov* at least twelve times and hopes someday to make it past page 152. *ecwhendren.wordpress.com*

 Amal Khan, originally of Lahore, Pakistan, always feels inspired in cities—the crowds, the lives, the strange noises of humans. She often feels nostalgic for places she has never been yet. Two degrees in politics helped show her all she wants is to be a writer. She dislikes speaking on the telephone and avoids it as much as possible. She believes kindness is the only human quality that can really change anything. *amal.skhan@gmail.com*

 Henry Mills stepped out from the cardboard transmogrifier as a human after spending his formative years as a horse only to discover eating Indian food, drinking tea, dual rectifiers, and other comforts make the world an easier place to be in. He spends too much time on Gmail, Facebook, and the BBC even after recognizing that his feelings of anxiety correlate to time spent on the Web. He has found the best remedy to be galloping in a big circle at shows or playing in bands with his friends. *www.myspace.com/henrymills*

Time You Let Me In

Jonah Ogles has a cat named Superwolf. He has worked as an editor in Beijing, China; a music teacher; and a gardener. He loves to go canoeing and take long walks. He hopes someday to build his own house in the woods and to have a dog named Bird.

When Tala Abu Rahmeh was little, she thought her mother was a magician. She had an imaginary friend called Zahra who loved red lunch boxes. Tala cries tears of happiness when she reads James Baldwin or Mahmoud Darwish. She washes her sheets just to smell laundry detergent on them, and loves cotton candy and the word "spectacular." She has walked down every street in Ramallah. She hopes to own her own art gallery to support young artists and poets by the time she is twenty-seven.

Allison Rivers comes from a family of law-enforcement officers, nurses, and pastors. She prefers singing opera to pop songs and likes sweatshirts, good jeans, and solo road trips. She has worked as a wedding coordinator on scenic Windmill Island, where a 240-year-old Dutch windmill continues to function.

Kayla Sargeson dislikes the consistency of mashed potatoes and has been afraid of escalators since birth. She likes Doritos Nacho Cheesier and Frida Kahlo and decorates her room with Frida greeting cards. In her free time, she collects Victoria's Secret bras. She has never had a driver's license.

Mary Selph wore out seven pairs of sneakers knocking on doors for grassroots political organizations. She is mildly obsessed with chipotle chiles and artichokes. She has frequent bouts of hiccups and describes herself as a "terrible singer and even worse dancer." It takes her a long time to write an e-mail.

Time You Let Me In

Lauren Stacks despises movies made from books. She worked for two years at an old-fashioned candy store and loves chocolate-covered potato chips. She will organize anything—sugar packets, closets, bookcases—and has on occasion been called obsessive compulsive. Her idea of a perfect morning is drinking coffee and working on a crossword puzzle. She finds it impossible to have a serious conversation without crying. Also, Lauren holds her high school's pole-vaulting record. *lauren-stacks.blogspot.com*

Jocelyn Stott repaints her living room every time a new can of clearance paint catches her eye: "There is something about commitment that terrifies me, so I practice committing to a wall color." A professor once told her that the pace of poetry is a walking pace. "Clumsy and awkwardly tall for most of my life, I enjoy discovering how the unresolved, uncomfortable and sometimes repulsive moments of memory can be made somehow graceful through writing."

230

Anna West has a weakness for chocolate and ice cream, a distaste for birthdays but an innate love of half birthdays, a tendency not to realize her own idiosyncrasies until she's disclosed them unwittingly in a room full of people, and unusual knees that do not look straight. She has taught poetry to inner-city kids.

Ben Westlie drives a Volkswagen Beetle named Jamal Beaverhausen and usually reads books in his car. He has a Lhasa apso who eats fruits and vegetables. He secretly wants to be a comedian, and often sings Disney songs while serving tables through his waiter shifts, just to make himself smile. He really loves getting mail in his mailbox and sometimes actually waits for the mail carrier.

Alexis D. Pepper-Smith lives on a British Columbian island.

NAOMI SHIHAB NYE has received a Lannan Fellowship, a Guggenheim Fellowship, the Witter Bynner Fellowship from the Library of Congress, and four Pushcart Prizes. Her collection *19 Varieties of Gazelle: Poems of the Middle East* was a finalist for the National Book Award, and her collection *Honeybee* was awarded the Arab–American Book Award. Naomi Shihab Nye has edited several honored and popular poetry anthologies, including *What Have You Lost?*, *Salting the Ocean*, and *This Same Sky*. She lives with her family in San Antonio, Texas.

ACKNOWLEDGMENTS

The individual poets represented in this volume hold the copyright to their poems. The compiler and the publisher gratefully acknowledge their permission to reprint the poems. A few of the poems have previously appeared elsewhere, as follows:

"foundling" by Matthew Baker first appeared in *The Lumberyard* (Issue 3).

"My Summer with the Norseman" by Margaret Bashaar first appeared in *Caketrain* (Issue 4: Fall/Winter 2006). It was also included in *Barefoot and Listening,* a chapbook published by Tilt Press, 2009.

"Through the Barn Doors" by Catherine Bates first appeared in *Southern Poetry Review* (45:1).

"On the Question of What Drives Coronary Circulation . . ." by Mario Chard first appeared in *Rattle* (Summer 2009).

231

INDEX OF POEMS

Time You Let Me In

233

Time You Let Me In

235

INDEX OF POETS